Dear mouse friends,
Welcome to the world of

Geronimo Stilton

THE RODENT'S GAZETTE
EDITORIAL STAFF

Geronimo Stilton
A learned and brainy
mouse; editor of
The Rodent's Gazette

Thea Stilton
Geronimo's sister and
special correspondent at
The Rodent's Gazette

Trap Stilton
An awful joker;
Geronimo's cousin and
owner of the store
Cheap Junk for Less

Benjamin Stilton
A sweet and loving
nine-year-old mouse;
Geronimo's favorite
nephew

Stilton

BOLLYWOOD BURGLARY

Scholastic Inc.

Copyright © 2015 by Edizioni Piemme S.p.A., Palazzo Mondadori, Via Mondadori 1, 20090 Segrate, Italy. International Rights © Atlantyca S.p.A. English translation © 2016 by Atlantyca S.p.A.

The publisher does not have any control over and does not assume any responsibility for author or third-party websites or their content.

GERONIMO STILTON names, characters, and related indicia are copyright, trademark, and exclusive license of Atlantyca S.p.A. All rights reserved. The moral right of the author has been asserted. Based on an original idea by Elisabetta Dami. www.geronimostilton.com

Published by Scholastic Inc., *Publishers since 1920*, 557 Broadway, New York, NY 10012. SCHOLASTIC and associated logos are trademarks and/or registered trademarks of Scholastic Inc.

Stilton is the name of a famous English cheese. It is a registered trademark of the Stilton Cheese Makers' Association. For more information, go to www. stiltoncheese.com.

No part of this publication may be reproduced, stored in a retrieval system, or transmitted in any form or by any means, electronic, mechanical, photocopying, recording, or otherwise, without written permission of the copyright holder. For information regarding permission, please contact: Atlantyca S.p.A., Via Leopardi 8, 20123 Milan, Italy; e-mail foreignrights@atlantyca.it, www. atlantyca.com.

ISBN 978-1-338-08775-8

Text by Geronimo Stilton
Original title *Il mistero del rubino d'Oriente*
Cover by Danilo Barozzi
Illustrations by Danilo Loizedda (design) and Daria Cerchi (color)
Graphics by Michela Battaglin

Special thanks to Beth Dunfey
Translated by Lidia Morson Tramontozzi
Interior design by Kay Petronio

10 9 8 7 6 5 4 3 2 1   17 18 19 20 21

Printed in the U.S.A.   40
First printing 2017

17 Spice Street

That **day** began like any other — it seemed like a **perfectly normal** day, in fact. But it turned out to be one of the most incredible, mousetastic days of my life! By the time I put my snout back on my pillow that night, my life had **CHANGED FOREVER**.

Oh, excuse me, I almost forgot to introduce myself. My name is Stilton, *Geronimo Stilton*, and I am the editor of *The Rodent's Gazette*, the most famouse newspaper on Mouse Island.

Yawn . . .

Mmm, hot cheese . . .

Oops!

Now, where was I? Oh yes! My morning began like any other . . .

I climbed out of bed and **scampered** to my office. Once I got settled at my desk, I started brainstorming. I had to come up with an idea for a new series of books. Hmm . . . should I write a book on **gardening**? Or *do-it-yourself* projects? Or **SPORTS**? Or . . .

I thought and thought and thought. By lunchtime, I was still thinking.

Hmm . . .

AND THEN SOMETHING STRANGE HAPPENED . . .

VISIT INDIA!

I glanced out the window, and there was a small plane towing a **BANNER** right outside — I mean, *right* outside — my office. VISIT INDIA! it said. Hmm, that was unusual!

The mailmouse came and left me ninety-four travel brochures about India. Hmm, that was a bit odd!

A second later, the phone rang and a **STRANGE** rodent squeaked, "My dear Mr. Stilton, how about a trip to India? I'll give you a discount . . ."

How strange!

"Thanks, but I think I'll pass," I answered.

Then I got an email with a *very* weird invitation . . .

3

MAILBOX   GET MAIL   NEW MESSAGE   PRINT   LABEL

TO: Geronimo Stilton

SUBJECT: A fabumouse invitation

FAVORITES   FIND   TOOLS   CHAT

A message for Mr. Stilton: Would you like to try a delectable assortment of delicious dishes? Come to the Taj Mahal Indian restaurant, 17 Spice Street. It'll be whisker-licking good!

Hmm, that was a wee bit bizarre!

But on the other paw, it was lunchtime, and I was hungry. I didn't want to think twice about food. So I hailed a **TAXI** and headed toward 17 Spice Street.

When my cab screeched up to the curb, I spotted a fabumouse **painted wooden door** and smelled an **intriguing** array of spices . . . **yummy, yum, yum!** It sure smelled whisker-licking good!

INDIAN FOOD

Indian cuisine includes a wide assortment of colors, aromas, and *flavors*.

Food from India's northern regions is non-vegetarian and less spicy, using more dairy products in dishes. The cuisine of the southern regions is mostly vegetarian and tends to be **spicier**.

Dishes are often flavored with **SPICES** like turmeric, coriander, cumin, and tamarind, also known as the "Indian date."

Rice is a staple food of India, and it is served hot as a side dish. When cooked in broth and flavored with spices, it's called *pilau*. When served with chicken, lamb, or vegetables, it's called **BIRYANI**.

Bread is also an essential staple, especially in the north. There are many varieties of bread. The most widespread in India is **ROTI** (also known as **CHAPATI**), an unleavened round bread made with whole-wheat flour.

DAL is a typical Indian dish that is creamy and made with lentils and various spices. There are many types of **DAL**.

STEAM'S COMING OUT OF MY EEEEEARS!

As soon as I entered the restaurant, a waiter with thick fur and shiny whiskers scurried over.

"Yoo-hoo! Welcome, my dear Stilton! Have you ever been to INDIA?" he asked.

"No, not yet," I answered.

"But that's absolutely elementary. You are thinking of GOING, then?" he said.

"Actually, no . . ." I replied.

"Actually, yes, you will be! **SOON!** Very, very soon. In fact, let's make a bet. I bet that you will go to India!"

Then the waiter waved a sheet of paper under my snout. "Now sign right here, Stilton!"

I was flabbergasted. No restaurant had ever asked me to pay my bill **BEFORE** I'd even ordered my meal! But I was hungrier than a rat in a cheese shop. I couldn't wait to sit down and eat, so I signed.

I took a better look at the waiter. There was something familiar about his snout. He also had a **squeaky** voice that

Sign here, Stilton!

Uhhhh . . . okay?

reminded me of someone . . .

"Have we met before?" I asked.

"NOOO, NOOOO!" the waiter replied. "Whatever gave you that idea, my dear Stilton?" He pushed me toward a table at the back of the room.

You remind me of someone!

The restaurant was lovely. The walls were covered with red silk **tapestries** embroidered in gold, and there was a **MOUSETASTIC** fountain in the center of the dining area. Delectable **aromas** and fabumouse Indian **music** filled the air. Waiters scurried around

with trays loaded with yummy dishes. I saw **chicken tikka masala** (chicken with creamy tomato sauce and spices) and **SAMoSAS** (stuffed fried pastries).

I glanced at the menu. "**Um, I'd like . . .**"

But the waiter ripped the menu out of my paws. "You **DON'T KNOW** much about Indian food, Mr. Stilton," he snorted. "Let me choose for you! **DO YOU LIKE SPICY FOOD?**"

"Um, yes, I do," I admitted. "But not *too* spicy . . ."

The waiter ran off, **SHOUtiNG**, "I'll bring you a meal that'll knock your tail off! It'll be **very hot**!"

As he disappeared into the kitchen, I heard him squeak, "A **spicy** one for the rodent in the rear! Heavy on the hot pepper. That'll make his whiskers do the **loop-the-loop**!"

Five minutes later, he returned with a tray of **steaming** dishes. "Try the one with the **hot pepper**!" he ordered.

I tasted the first dish. It was **HOT**!

I tasted the second. It was **VERY HOT**!

Then I tasted the third dish. It was **EXTREMELY HOT**!

I wanted to stop, but the waiter kept shoveling spoonfuls into my snout.

"Let's see **HOW MUCH** this customer can take before he **BURSTS**!" he cried gleefully.

I couldn't take it anymore.

"One more bite, Stilton," he insisted. "By the time you're in **India**, you'll be used to **hot peppers**."

"But I'm not going to India!" I protested.

"But you *will* go to India," he insisted. "Wanna bet on it?"

When he shoved a dollop from dish

HOT!

VERY HOT!

VERY, VERY HOT!

OUCHIE! MY TONGUE IS BURNING!

MY MOUTH IS ON FIRE!

number ten into my mouth, STEAM started coming out of my ears.

SMOKIN' SAMOSAS, THAT WAS ONE FUR-RAISING HOT PEPPER!

6 — MY TONSILS ARE SCORCHED!

7 — IT'S SO HOT I CAN'T BREATHE!

8 — HEEELP! MY BELLY IS ABLAZE!

9 — I'M AS RED AS A RIPE HOT PEPPER!

10 — STEAM'S COMING OUT OF MY EARS!

"I'm **BURNING UP**!" I screeched.

I ran to the fountain and dunked my whole head into it.

I heard a sizzle.

FZzZzZzZZZZZZ!

I'm burning uuuup!

What's the matter with him?

When I returned to my table, the waiter asked, "So when are we going to India?"

"I'm too busy, okay?" I shouted. "B-u-s-y! Very busy! I can't possibly go to India!"

DON'T BE A FLY IN THE FONDUE!

The waiter was disappointed. "Geronimo, you're such a **FUR-BRAIN**!" he scolded me. "I was really hoping you'd go to India with me . . ."

And that's when I recognized him.

"You're not a waiter. You're . . . my detective friend, Hercule Poirat!" I cried.

Ha, ha, ha!

It's you, Hercule Poirat!

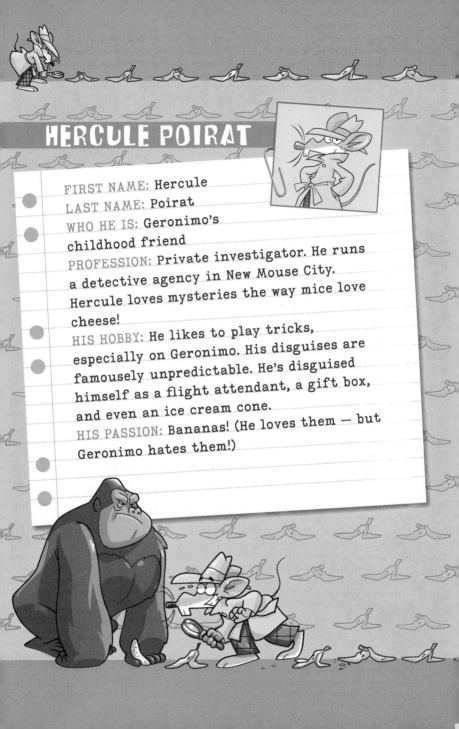

HERCULE POIRAT

FIRST NAME: Hercule

LAST NAME: Poirat

WHO HE IS: Geronimo's childhood friend

PROFESSION: Private investigator. He runs a detective agency in New Mouse City. Hercule loves mysteries the way mice love cheese!

HIS HOBBY: He likes to play tricks, especially on Geronimo. His disguises are famously unpredictable. He's disguised himself as a flight attendant, a gift box, and even an ice cream cone.

HIS PASSION: Bananas! (He loves them — but Geronimo hates them!)

Poirat pulled off his **WIG** and **ripped** the slick mustache from his snout.

"Yes, it is I: Poirat, Hercule Poirat! And you simply must go to India with me."

I shook my snout. "I can't go to India with you. I'm too busy, Hercule! I've told you over and over again!"

Poirat started to sob. "Yes, my dear Stilton. You did tell me . . . several times, in

Please, please, please!

No way! I can't go.

fact . . . but I need your help! Please! I'm begging you!"

I rolled my eyes. Poirat must have noticed, because he changed tactics. He dried his tears on my jacket sleeve and **BLEW** his nose on my tie. "So do you have your passport on you?" he asked calmly. "We could leave right now!"

By this time, I was annoyed. "I'm sorry. But I simply cannot go!"

"My dear Stilton, why must you be so stubborn?!" he squeaked loudly. "Don't you **W A N T** to go to Indiaaaa?"

Every snout in the restaurant turned to look at me. "Is that Geronimo Stilton? Why doesn't he want to go to India? Does he dislike India? But why?"

"No, it's not . . . I don't have anything against India — I'm sure I'd love it there!

I just . . ." I cried in exasperation.

"He said he'd love it there!" Hercule shouted. **FASTER** than the mouse who ran up the clock, he reached into my pocket and pulled out my PASSPORT.

"How positively banana-rific! You and I are going to India, Gerrykins. Don't be such a **fly in the fondue**! You've run out of excuses. Look, I found your passport!"

"You still haven't said **WHY** I have to go to India," I shouted. "Can you please just tell me?!"

He pulled out a photo and glanced at it MYSTERIOUSLY. "Do you recognize this rodent? Look closely!"

Mouse Island

I saw the *beautiful* snout of an Indian mouselet I didn't recognize.

"It's Ratna!" Hercule squeaked.

I can't go, but I'm sure I'd love India!

Did you hear that?

Yeah! Go figure!

"Ratna!? Dear Ratna . . ." I repeated. A million memories flooded my snout.

Ratna was an old and dear friend from mouselinghood. She and Hercule and I had attended Little Tails Academy together. It was a SAD day for us when she and her family moved back to India!

Ratna!

So many memories!

In School

Ratna's birthday

Friends forever!

THE HEART OF FIRE

"My dear Stilton, don't you remember? We promised we'd be FRIENDS FOREVER. Me, you, and Ratna!" Hercule squeaked.

"Yes, of course I remember . . .

and i always keep my promises.

What's that got to do with India?" I asked.

Poirat chuckled. "Everything, Gerrykins," he said. "Don't damage your little gray cells, old friend! Simply use your EYEBALLS and take a good look at the ruby in the photo."

He showed me a magazine with a photo of an enormouse heart-shaped ruby. It was magnificent — so brilliant RED, so dazzling!

"Ratna's fiancé gave her this ruby as

an engagement gift," Poirat explained.

"That's quite a gift!" I exclaimed. "It must be **priceless**!"

Poirat **SIGHED**. "Since **Ratna** has had the ruby, there have been several attempts to steal it.

See this ruby?

It's priceless!

THE HEART OF FIRE

This amazing gem is absolutely unique! It is renowned for its heart shape, its blazing red color, and its exceptional clarity!

The ruby belonged for generations to the Maharaja of Rajasthan. It was recently purchased by the famouse Bollywood actor, Vinay Ratingh, for his equally famouse fiancåe, Ratna Prem.

The ruby has a long history. Because it's so valuable, it has always been an irresistible target for thieves.

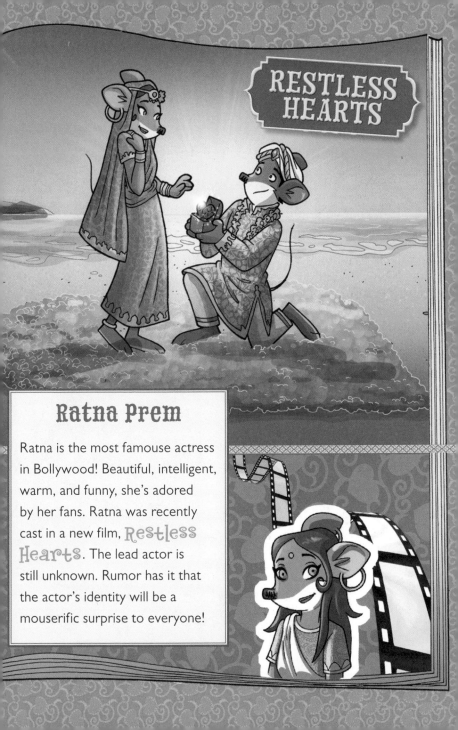

RESTLESS HEARTS

Ratna Prem

Ratna is the most famouse actress in Bollywood! Beautiful, intelligent, warm, and funny, she's adored by her fans. Ratna was recently cast in a new film, Restless Hearts. The lead actor is still unknown. Rumor has it that the actor's identity will be a mouserific surprise to everyone!

That's why she wants us to travel around India with her during the shoot for her next film, Restless Hearts. She needs PROTECTION, and she wants to make sure no rodent with sticky paws tries to steal her ruby. I've already promised her we would come."

He showed me the email Ratna sent asking us to help.

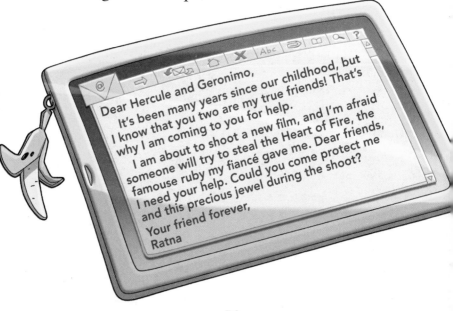

Dear Hercule and Geronimo,
It's been many years since our childhood, but I know that you two are my true friends! That's why I am coming to you for help.
I am about to shoot a new film, and I'm afraid someone will try to steal the Heart of Fire, the famouse ruby my fiancé gave me. Dear friends, I need your help. Could you come protect me and this precious jewel during the shoot?
Your friend forever,
Ratna

"Why didn't you just tell me that this was all to **HELP** Ratna?" I scolded Hercule. "Of course I will help! Ratna is an old friend. And true friendship is as rare as fine cheddar."

"Ahem, there's just one more thing you should know, my dear Stilton . . ." Poirat **mumbled**.

I looked at him suspiciously. "What is it? Spit it out!"

Poirat looked sheepish. "Well, you see, I also told Ratna that you'd, um, be acting alongside her in the film . . . That way, we'll have someone undercover and no one will be able to steal the ruby," he added quickly. "It was a genius idea, right, Gerrykins?"

He took out his MousePhone and showed me an article about the new movie.

MY EYES ALMOST POPPED

OUT OF THEIR SOCKETS. THERE WAS A BIG PICTURE OF . . . ME!

It was the poster for the BOLLYWOOD movie, and it had been distributed all over India!

"*Restless Hearts*, starring Ratna Prem and Geronimo Stilton," I read. "But . . . but . . . but . . . I don't know how to act! I can't possibly be the lead mouse in a film! I won't do it!"

Hercule coughed. "Ahem, Gerrykins, I'm afraid you've already *signed* the contract with the movie producer."

"Spicy cheese dip, I certainly did not sign a contract!" I protested.

Hercule giggled. "Oh yes, you certainly did!"

Hercule handed me the paper that I had previously assumed was the restaurant's bill,

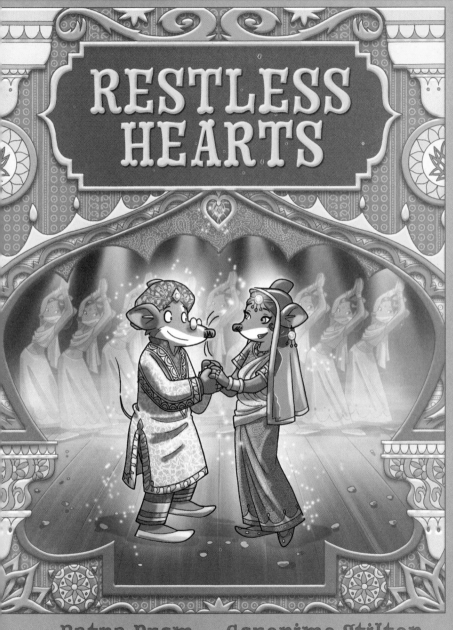

RESTLESS HEARTS

STARRING **Ratna Prem** AND **Geronimo Stilton**

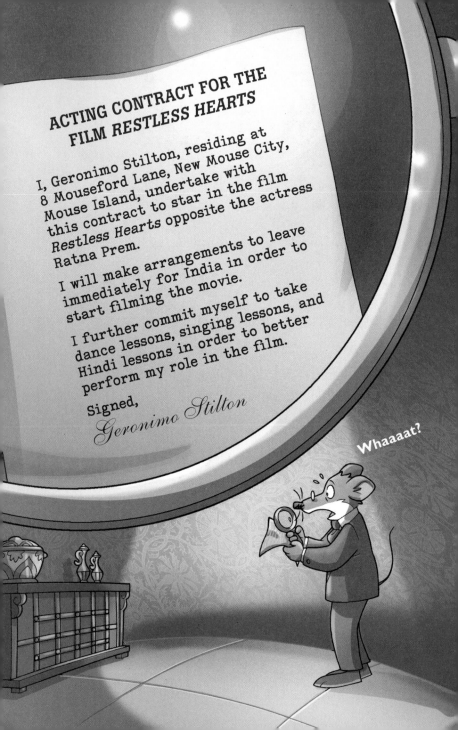

along with an enormouse MAGNIFYING glass so I could examine it.

"Nooooo! I really did sign it!" I cried in despair.

"Yeees! You really diiiid!" Hercule squeaked happily. He waved two airline tickets under my snout. "I've already bought the tickets to India. We're leaving today! Aren't you excited, Gerrykins?"

Noooooo!

We must leave immediately!

Sob!

OFF TO INDIA!

What could I do? The idea of being in a movie was totally terrifying . . . but it was all to **HELP** an old friend. So how could I refuse?

Even though so many years had gone by, Ratna still held a special place in my heart.

At the very least, I was looking forward to seeing her! I packed my **suitcase** and headed to the airport with Hercule.

The trip was very long, and Hercule **blabbed** the entire time. First he **tOLD** me the plot of Restless Hearts in great detail . . .

RESTLESS HEARTS

MAIN CHARACTERS:

Ratna Prem in the role of a princess of Rajasthan
Geronimo Stilton in the role of the prince of Mysore

PLOT:

It is a time long ago. The prince of Mysore sees a miniature portrait of the beautiful princess of Rajasthan and instantly falls in love with her.

The prince writes the princess a letter and sends her priceless gifts, but she takes no notice. So, hoping to impress her, he decides to go on a quest of amazing feats.

First, he explores the Indian jungle and is nearly devoured by a Bengal tiger. Then he goes to Varanasi to collect the sacred waters of the Ganges River for her. Next, he gallops to Jaipur, Rajasthan — the romantic Pink City where the princess lives.

There the princess and prince meet, and he convinces her to visit the Taj Mahal with him. It is there, by this legendary monument and symbol of love, that he declares his love. And the princess finally agrees to marry him!

Hercule and I were sitting next to each other, so there was no escape. He read me a SUPER-MEGA-HUGE guidebook of India from cover to cover!

We finally LANDED in New Delhi, the Indian capital city.

By that time, I was so worried about the film that my EYES were wider than wheels of cheese. But at least I knew

I can't take it!

practically everything about India!

As soon as the PLANE'S hatch opened, a wave of hot, humid air greeted us. It smelled of FLOWERS and spices. I could see the city's skyline in the distance.

I have to admit it . . . I was also so excited, I was practically jumping out of my fur. You see, I love to travel. And I had always longed to visit India.

We were in India . . . one of the most fascinating countries in the world!

Our trip had just begun, but my heart was already beating faster than a hamster on a wheel. We were going to have an amazing ADVENTURE!

Official Name: Republic of India; Bharat, in Hindi

Area: 1,269,300 square miles

Population: 1,299,490,000 inhabitants (2015 estimate)

Capital: New Delhi

Official Languages: Hindi and English

Type of Government: Federal republic

Currency: Indian rupee

Climate: India has four seasons: The winter season lasts from January to February, with mild, sunny days and cold nights in the north. Summer, or pre-monsoon season, lasts from March to May, with high and humid temperatures, except in the mountains. The southwest monsoon season, or rainy season, lasts from July to September. Post-monsoon season is October to December and marks the transition from wet to dry conditions.

Geography: The snowy peaks and deep valleys of the Himalayas and the vast plains of the Ganges River are found in northern India. In the south lies a plateau called the Deccan. It is flanked by the Eastern and Western Ghats, mountains that run parallel to the eastern and western coasts.

Time Zones: Although India is very large, the entire country follows one time zone, known informally as Indian Standard Time. India does not observe Daylight Saving Time.

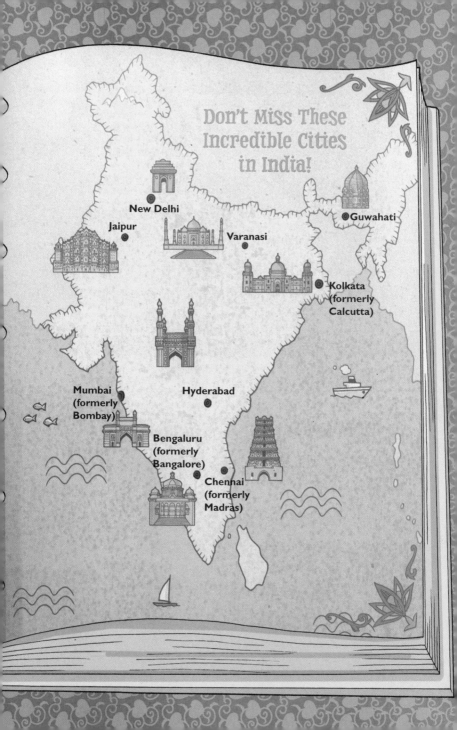

RESTLESS HEARTS

As soon as we arrived in NEW DELHI, Hercule stuffed me, my achy tail, and all our suitcases inside a **TAXI**. "Scurry up, my dear Stilton! They're waiting for us!"

The taxi dropped us in front of an ENORMOUSE theater. Outside, there was a SiGN that read:

Screen tests
for the movie
RESTLESS HEARTS

FILM CREW ONLY!

"We can go in here, Gerrykins. You're the lead **actor**," Hercule said, SMIRKING under his whiskers.

Dear reader, I'm a very shy mouse. Why, just the thought of squeaking in public makes me blush to the roots of my fur. How in the name of string cheese was I going to act in front of a movie camera?

"Er . . . I changed my mind. I-I'm going home," I stammered.

Hercule grabbed me by the tail. "What about Ratna? Some friend you turned out to be!"

Squeak!

I thought of Ratna and sighed. She was my friend. I couldn't abandon her! So I scampered into the theater.

All the lights were off except for the spotlight on the STAGE, which was shining on a group of dancers. They were all singing in chorus:

"He could feel . . . that they were drifting apart.
He understood . . that he had been mistaken.
Alas, he had never had her heart . . .
Alas, alas, alas . . . he was forsaken!"

Besides the DANCERS, there were dozens of other rodents in the theater, busily scurrying to and fro. Poirat pointed out each one to me.

"That's the director! And that's his assistant! That mouselet is the COSTUME DESIGNER . . . that's the makeup artist, and that's . . ."

WELCOME TO INDIA, MR. STILTON

"Welcome to India, Mr. Stilton!" someone behind me squeaked.

I turned and saw a mouse with an extremely long braid. "I'm Vandana Ratkita, the casting director* for *Restless Hearts*," she said in a gentle tone.

She **LOOKED** me over from the tip of my ears to the tip of my tail. "Now, Mr. Stilton, you are playing the prince of Mysore: You'll be AMAZING — PERFECT — incredible!"

---

* The casting director selects actors for all the parts in a film.

Vandana pushed me toward the stage. "Let me see how you dance, Mr. Stilton!"

I turned **REDDER** than a cheese rind. "Erm, I don't know . . . I mean, I haven't got a clue how to, um, dance!"

The dancers turned to stare at me. Then they began murmuring, "Did you hear that? HE DOESN'T KNOW HOW TO DANCE!"

Suddenly, the theater was so quiet, you could hear a cheese slice drop. The director,

DEV MOUSEPALI, slapped me on the back so hard my tailbone rattled. "So what if he doesn't know how to dance? He'll learn!" he cried. "**MRS. RATEL** will teach him!"

Everyone let out a **SIGH** of relief. "Yeah, Mrs. Ratel will take care of him. She'll teach him everything he needs to know. He better learn, or. . ."

"Or what?" I cried, twisting my tail. "I need to know. Tell me!"

HE DOESN'T KNOW HOW TO DANCE!

But they ignored me and went back to their dancing. They LEAPED here and there to the beat of the music. They were so graceful! I knew I'd never be able to dance like that . . .

Hercule DRAGGED me away to my trailer. "Sleep tight, my dear Stilton!" he told me. "You need your rest. Tomorrow you'll be shaking your tail and prancing your paws off!"

HE DOESN'T KNOW HOW TO DANCE!

Ack!

CREAM FOR THE CALLUSES

The long trip from Mouse Island had worn me out. I closed my **EYES** and fell deeply asleep . . .

Zzzz . . . zzzzz zzzzzz!

At dawn the following morning, Hercule woke me up by shrieking directly into my left ear. "Wake up, my dear Stilton! Shake a paw! It's time to get your tail moving!"

My **PAWS** had barely touched the floor, when Hercule poured a scalding **CUP** of tea down my throat. It was so hot it burned my gullet! Then he shoved a handful of CANDY into my snout.

"Here's some hot-pepper candy. I added

more HOT PEPPERS to give it extra zip. Like it, Gerrykins?" he demanded.

"Aaaarghhh!" I screeched. The hot-pepper candies had gone down the wrong way, and I almost choked!

cough! cough! cough!

"A quick shower will perk you up. It'll help you move those PAWS to the beat, Stilton!" squeaked Hercule, pushing me into a cold shower.

"HEEEELP! You're going to freeze my tail off!" I cried.

So he turned the faucet,

Drink this tea!

Eat these candies!

and instantly the water became boiling **hot**!

"Noooooo!" I screeched. "Now you're scorching the fur right off my back!"

"*Come on, Gerrykins*, why do you have to be so difficult?" he complained. "You're never happy!"

The STEAM in the shower was so thick I couldn't see my paw in front of my snout. I felt around for the shampoo, toothpaste, and fur-gel. But the shampoo wouldn't **lather**, the toothpaste tasted worse

I brushed my teeth WITH SHAMPOO . . .

What a mess! I washed my fur WITH TOOTHPASTE . . .

than day-old tuna, and the gel matted my **fur** like a mangy marmot!

SQUEAK!

I had washed my fur with toothpaste,
brushed my teeth with shampoo,
and combed my fur with callus cream!

"Ha, ha, ha! At least you won't have any calluses in your fur!" Hercule *giggled*.

The day had started out **all wrong** . . . I was afraid to think about how it would end!

I definitely STARTED THE DAY ON THE WRONG PAW!

SIGH!
SIGH!

And I combed my fur
with CALLUS CREAM!

MR. STILTON'S DREADFUL DAY

Priya Moushi, the costume designer, brought me my costume: a **SILK** tunic, a pair of bright green pants, and a marvemouse **TURBAN** with a jewel.

Once I was dressed, the **Makeup artist** came to put on my makeup. After she was finished, she led me into a big room with wooden floors. Waiting for me there was my *dance* teacher, **SIDDHI RATEL**.

I'm on it!

Mrs. Ratel was an elderly rodent with snow-white fur gathered into a tight **BUN**. She wore a pink **sari*** and held a wooden stick in her paw.

* A sari is a garment worn by many Indian women made of a long cloth wrapped around so one end forms a skirt and the other goes over the shoulder.

She had a very SEVERE expression on her snout.

"Mr. Stilton, my name is **Siddhi**, which means '*perfection*,'" she squeaked sternly. "And I expect you to learn how to dance *perfectly*!" Then she rapped me on the tail with the stick. CLONK!

"Now for your first dance lesson, Mr. Stilton! One . . . two . . . three . . . What are you doing? Are you sleepwalking? Mr. Stilton, you're about as graceful as a goat!"

"Mrs. Ratel, I must warn you. I'm a truly lost cause," I told her. "I can't dance! My Aunt Sweetfur always says I was born with two left paws."

Mrs. Ratel didn't listen. She just CLONKED me on the tail again. CLONK!

"Young mouse, I've been teaching for the last fifty years. There's no such thing as a **LOST CAUSE**. Come on, hop to it! One . . . two . . . three!"

Every time I **MESSED UP** a step, she whacked me on the tail. **CLONK!**

"**YEE-OUCH!**" I yelled.

After hours and hours of (useless) practice, Mrs. Ratel **gave up**. She broke her wooden stick over her knee in frustration.

It's impossible to teach you to dance!

Um . . . actually . . . well . . . squeeeak!

"You're right, Mr. Stilton. You're truly a lost cause. I give up! It's impossible to teach you to dance!"

Everyone on the set — from the DIRECTOR to the costume designer to the LIGHTING designer — was horrified.

"Are you sure? He can't be taught how to dance?" the director gasped.

Mrs. Ratel shook her snout.

"I TRIED ALL DAY, BUT HE'S A LOST CAUSE! HE CAN'T LEARN! AND IF I CAN'T TEACH HIM, I DON'T KNOW WHO CAN!"

"Uh, so what can I do? Can I GO HOME?" I said hopefully. "Can I pack my bags? Should I book my plane ticket?"

RATNA THE RAVISHING

That's when I heard a sweet voice squeak, "Don't worry, Geronimo! I'll teach you to dance. It's me, your old friend Ratna!"

I turned and saw a stunning mouselet. Her SOFT fur was a delicate hazelnut color, her eyes were as GREEN as emeralds, and her lips were the color of coral. Her long hair reached to her

She's beautiful!

She's unique!

What an actress!

Wow!

She's a star!

So charming!

My dear friends!

waist like a curtain of shiny silk. She wore an EMBROIDERED golden sari and a sparkly DIADEM* on her forehead.

"Ratna . . . it's really you!" I said.

She glided toward me with the *graceful* motions of a born dancer. "Geronimo, my dear friend. Thank you for coming to my aid."

Then she turned to Hercule. "Thank you, darling Hercule. It's so lovely having you here with me! I feel safe knowing my two oldest friends are looking out for me."

Ratna put her paw on my shoulder. "Just follow me, Geronimo. That's all you have to do. I'll teach you to dance," she squeaked softly.

---

* A diadem is an ornamental headband worn as a badge of royalty.

Musicians began to play on the **SiTAR**, a traditional Indian **STRINGED** instrument. The gentleness of the melody washed over me. Ratna sang along sweetly. Soon I was completely relaxed.

I followed Ratna's lead, **IMITATING** her movements, first slowly and then more and more swiftly. And that's how I learned to dance. Before long, I felt as if my paws were flying across the floor!

The director and the cast and crew all clapped.

"Bravo, Geronimo! Do it again!"

Next, Ratna taught me to sing in Hindi. When I followed her SWEET and melodic squeak, the words of that **unfamiliar**

language became easier to pronounce.
  Over the next few days, **Ratna** helped
me discover many things about India.

THE MORE I GOT
TO KNOW INDIA,
THE MORE I LIKED IT!

That's it!

Now you're dancing like a star!

Hercule grinned gleefully. "**See, Gerrykins**, what did I tell you? I knew you'd enjoy our trip to India! It's positively banana-rific!"

A Trip
Through India

After a few days of rehearsal, the entire crew **left** to start shooting the movie. The director, Dev, gave me a map of all the places we'd visit. **First**, we had to go to Sundarbans National Park in West Bengal. Then we'd head to the **jungle** — my character had to explore until I found a tiger . . .

A TIGER? THUNDERING CAT TAILS!

Next I had to **dive** into the Ganges in Varanasi and swim in that enormouse, raging river! I hoped I'd be brave enough to do it!

After that, I had to ride a horse to Jaipur. *Gulp* . . . did they expect me to GALLOP?

A chill went down my tail. I have a horrible history of motion sickness!

Finally, I had to go to the Taj Mahal in Agra and **DECLARE MY LOVE** to Ratna. I chewed my whiskers nervously. Would I be able to play the part of a lovesick rodent? You see, I'm a very shy mouse!

When we got to the jungle, I tried to hide in my trailer, but Hecule gave me a push.

"Quiet on the set!" the director shouted. "Action! Mr. Stilton, please come in from the jungle **LOOKING** courageous — bold — daring. And smile as if you don't know that this is a **DANGEROUS** place, famouse for its *wild* tigers . . ."

Help!

Take one!
Action!

"Oh, Mr. Stilton, wouldn't it be moustastic if a big, **hungry tiger** jumped out of the jungle?!" the assistant director **squealed**. "If we're lucky, you'll run into one, Mr. Stilton! Um, just to double-check . . . you've written your will, right?"

My will? Squeak! I almost passed out from fright! You see, I am a total SCAREDY-RAT.

I tried to sneak away, but Hercule **grabbed** me by the tail.

"Nuh-uh, Gerrykins. Don't make me look like a cheeseface. Go on! Take a little stroll in the jungle and *maybe you'll run into a teensy little tiger!*"

That's when I heard a growl.

GRRRRRRRR!

It almost sounded like . . . no, actually, in fact — there was absomousely no doubt about it . . . it was **the roar of a tiger**!

There was a real TIGER right on my tail! I began to **RUN** as fast as my paws could carry me.

For a moment, I slowed down as I thought about how happy the assistant director must be. Then I began scampering my tail off again!

As I scurried away, a little monkey threw a banana at my snout. **Boink!**

But an angry monkey was the least of my problems. My tail twitching with terror, I finally reached my trailer and **LOCKED** myself in.

The assistant director KNOCKED at the door. "Mr. Stilton, we have to **reshoot**

that entire scene. We were so excited about the tiger, we forgot to turn on the **movie camera**! So we need to take it from the top, from the moment the tiger begins chasing you. Are you **READY**, Mr. Stilton?"

Eek!

WHAT HAPPENED TO MY BANANAS?

When we finished **FILMING** the scene with the tiger, I went back to my **TRAILER** and found my door wide open.

WHO HAD OPENED IT?

Someone had climbed on top of the trailer and left strange **PAWPRINTS** all over the roof . . .

Who's been in my trailer?

Whose prints are those?

Whoever it was stole the fake rings I kept in my jewelry case and DEVOURED all of Hercule's bananas. How strange!

"If I find the THIEF who ate my bananas, I'll make mousemeat of him!" Hercule shrieked. "You play with the rat, you get the tail!"

Then we discovered that objects had disappeared from the other actors' trailers,

Who stole my chocolates?

too . . . especially objects that were SPARKLY!

Fruit and TREATS were also missing. And wherever there was a theft, we found the same strange **PAWPRiNTS**, not just on the floor and furniture, but also on the roof.

Who ate my bananas?

"I hate to say it, but there's a thief on the loose," I squeaked.

"**RATS!** Well, the important thing is that this fur-face doesn't steal the **HEART OF FIRE**," said Hercule.

Who stole my belt?

Just to be on the safe side, we **doubled** the surveillance on **Ratna** and her ruby. Anytime she went anywhere, we went with her. We were

determined to **PROTECT HER**.

The next morning, we left for Varanasi at dawn. From there, we continued on to **JAIPUR** and then to **AGRA**.

When the time came to *shoot* the FINAL SCENE, where the prince declares his love in front of the Taj Mahal, I was very nervous. I knelt before Ratna and squeaked, "Princess of Rajasthan, will you marry me?"

"Yes, oh, prince of Mysore, I will!" she WHISPERED.

The orchestra swelled, and all the DANCERS began to dance.

This was our spectacular grand finale — and the end of the movie shoot!

"How did I do?" I asked *anxiously*.

The cast and crew applauded. "You were amazing, Mr. Stilton! Bravo!"

Great job!

I went back to my trailer to take off my makeup and **turBan**. Hercule followed me.

Ratna joined us in the trailer a few minutes later. "You've been **FABUMOUSE**, my friends!" she cried. "Because of you, I have felt so safe and secure these past few weeks. And thanks to you, no one has stolen the **HEART OF FIRE**!"

Plink!

Plink!

Plink!

I smiled. "We're so happy we could help you, Ratna."

Hercule nodded. "Would you like a banana?"

"No thanks, Hercule, but I would like to ask you one last favor," she continued. "My fiancé and I have set our **wedding** date, and it's to take place in Mumbai in a few days.

Will you come to my wedding?

Of course!

Yes! Fabumouse!

Since you are my oldest and dearest friends, I would love for you to be guests of honor at our wedding!"

We accepted **happily**. And then we PACKED our bags for Mumbai . . . the famouse movie capital of India!

BOLLYWOOD

The word *Bollywood* comes from two words: *Hollywood* plus *Bombay*, the old name for Mumbai. Today Mumbai is the center of the Indian film industry. The music and dance that are a fundamental part of Indian culture are very important in Ratna's movie.

A CURIOUS CLUE

When we got to Mumbai, Vinay Ratingh, Ratna's fiancé, came to meet us. The two mice hugged joyously.

"Vinay, these are my oldest friends," Ratna squeaked.

Squeak!

My darling!

Aw, how sweet . . .

They're so happy together!

He bowed. "Your friends are my friends, darling!" He kissed her paw. "Come, we have to scurry up! Everything's ready for the wedding."

He escorted us to the most beautiful hotel in Mumbai. The preparations for the wedding reception were in full swing! Ratna and Vinay had invited A THOUSAND GUESTS. We saw a looooong table set up in the hall.

"Wow, a thousand guests? This reception is totally mouserageous!"

Hercule exclaimed.

Ratna scampered off for a quick ratnap. Tomorrow was a very big day — for her, and for all of us.

The following morning, Ratna MARRIED Vinay Ratingh. SHE LOOKED ABSOLUTELY RADIANT! The HEART OF FIRE sparkled from the front of her silk sari.

After the ceremony, there was a fabumouse dinner with a thousand happy guests.

The wedding cake was whisker-licking good. A statue of two miniature dancing mice twirled on top, but they didn't distract Hercule. He couldn't wait to taste a big bite! YUM, YUM, YUMMY!

We feasted all day, but DUSK came at last. The sun began slowly began to set, spreading its golden rays over the roofs of Mumbai.

It was time for the bride and groom to dance their first dance. The ballroom quickly filled with elegant rodents dressed in brightly colored silks, chatting merrily in many different languages.

The **HALL** was on the thirtieth floor, and the view of Mumbai was spectacular. Oh, how brightly the lights of the city twinkled!

It was the last night of our stay in India.

Good times!

You said it!

Hercule and I were **happy** the shoot was over, but sad to be leaving India so soon. We began REMINISCING about our favorite parts of the trip.

Hercule in particular was puffed up with pride. "See, my dear Stilton? Why it's absolutely elementary! No CROOK stole the ruby! We thwarted the thief! We foiled the felon!"

The squeaks had barely left his snout when a shriek broke the night.

"THE HEART OF FIRE HAS BEEN STOLEN!" Ratna cried.

We scampered to Ratna's side and found our friend in tears. "I had the ruby around my neck," she whimpered. "I danced with many guests. And then when I sat down with my GROOM, I realized I was no longer wearing the necklace."

"That crook tricked us! He hoodwinked us — he **bamboozled** us!" cried Hercule.

"Don't despair. You can count on us," I said firmly. "*We'll catch that thief!*"

Hercule nodded. "Have no fear, Hercule Poirat is here!" he cried.

Together, we turned to face the guests.

"EVERYONE FREEZE! NOBODY MOVE. NO RODENT SETS A PAW OUTSIDE THIS ROOM!"

Hercule searched the room while I searched the guests.

But the ruby was nowhere to be found. Where could it have gone?

As we looked for clues, we noticed a strange set of **PAWPRINTS** on the bride and groom's table. The prints led to a big picture window. They MATCHED the prints I'd found on my trailer during the shoot!

The window was wide open, and a gentle *BREEZE* made the curtains sway to and fro. I looked out the window and noticed a very narrow ledge below it. The pawprints continued onto the ledge, and then onto the gutter.

Maybe the thief had *JUMPED* to another **ROOF**, and from there, had hung from the gutter . . . and then had jumped from window to window until he disappeared!

Hmm . . . we were on the thirtieth floor. What kind of rat burglar could jump from that height?

A CRAFTY CROOK

I looked around and noticed something strange. There was a tuft of fur caught in the lock of the window! And a BANANA PEEL lay on the ledge.

Hmm. The thief had to be small, since no one had seen him NEAR Ratna. He was very agile, since he had leaped out the window from the thirtieth floor. He was losing tufts of fur, and he was obviously very fond of bananas . . .

I thought about the PAWPRINTS I had found on the trailers . . . and about the shiny

Some fur!

objects that had gone missing . . . and all of Hercule's bananas that the mysterious thief had gnawed on.

Then I remembered the little monkey that had bonked me on my head with a **BANANA** back when the **tiger** was *CHASING* me through the jungle. That was the day I'd found the door to my trailer wide **OPEN**. That's when all the robberies had begun!

Look!   Hmm . . .

Suddenly, I had an **INSPIRATION**. "By cheese, I think I've got it! Our pickpocket is a primate! Our crafty crook is a monkey!" I squeaked. "The problem is

catching him — and finding the **HEART OF FIRE**."

The monkey could be anywhere, and we had no idea where he'd hidden the Heart of Fire.

But Hercule had a plan. "I'm going to need the power of potassium! *Quickly, bring me all the bananas you can find!*" he shouted to the waiters.

The waiters scurried away. A few moments later, there was an **enormouse** pile of bananas in front of Hercule.

He began peeling one banana after another. Soon the air was filled with the sweet *scent* of fresh bananas.

I was starting to figure out what he was up to. Sometimes he thinks of some pretty **ingenious** ideas!

"Open all the windows! And **TURN**

OFF the lights," he ordered.

As soon as the room was **DARK**, Hercule squeaked, "And now everyone . . . hush!"

All the wedding guests froze, and the room **FELL** silent. The only sound was the *BREEZE* swishing through the open windows.

Suddenly, we made out a **SHAPE** on the ledge of the window. Nimbly it leaped into the room.

"Turn on the lights!" Hercule shouted.

As soon as the **LIGHTS** clicked on, we saw . . .

a little monkey wearing the

HEART OF FIRE

around its neck!

Hercule gently pawed him a banana.

"Hi, little one. Wanna trade?" he said softly. "A banana for the RUBY."

The monkey didn't hesitate. He placed the ruby in Hercule's open paw and took the banana.

Hercule proudly presented the Heart of Fire to Ratna.

"Thank you, my friends. I knew I could count on you!" Ratna cried, hugging him.

Here, have a banana.

Ooo! Ooo!

A FABUMOUSE IDEA

When I returned to New Mouse City, *Restless Hearts* was already playing in movie theaters . . . and *it was a ratastic success*! There were long lines in front of all the **theaters** in town.

The movie's success had set off a craze for anything **Indian**. All across New Mouse City, Indian-style clothing, music, and food were more **POPULAR** than Parmesan pastries.

I went to the office and sat gloomily at my desk. The trip to India had been a fabumouse diversion, but I still hadn't come up with an idea for a new series of books.

I tried to concentrate. Hmm . . . Should I publish books on gardening? Or on do-it-yourself projects? Or on sports? Maybe...

I was completely focused on picking a topic when Hercule BOUNDED into my office.

"My dear Stilton, what are you up to? Still thinking of our old pal Ratna?"

"Shh! Zip it! Shut your snout! I'm

Look! It's Geronimo! What an actor! So stylish! So charming! So classy!

trying to concentrate!" I grumbled.

"Are you as **concentrated** as a can of cheese-and-banana soup? Hee, hee, hee!" he **giggled**. "I've got an idea. *Just a teensy little idea!*" he exclaimed. "Why don't you write a series of books on food eaten around the world, starting with India?"

I had to admit, it was a really good idea! And that's how I came to publish a series of cookbooks called *Goodness from Around the Globe.*

The books were a **huge success**. It's great to eat the **traditional** food of your own country, but it's also great to discover flavors traditional to other cultures. Variety is the spice of life! **That's what's so great about diversity!**

And that's the truth, or my name isn't *Geronimo Stilton*!

TRADITIONS ARE WONDERFUL!

AND DISCOVERING THE TRADITIONS OF DIFFERENT RODENTS IN FARAWAY COUNTRIES IS WONDERFUL, TOO!

Especially when it comes to cooking and eating delicious foods!

Rodent's honor!

Be sure to read all my fabumouse adventures!

#1 Lost Treasure of the Emerald Eye

#2 The Curse of the Cheese Pyramid

#3 Cat and Mouse in a Haunted House

#4 I'm Too Fond of My Fur!

#5 Four Mice Deep in the Jungle

#6 Paws Off, Cheddarface!

#7 Red Pizzas for a Blue Count

#8 Attack of the Bandit Cats

#9 A Fabumouse Vacation for Geronimo

#10 All Because of a Cup of Coffee

#11 It's Halloween, You 'Fraidy Mouse!

#12 Merry Christmas, Geronimo!

#13 The Phantom of the Subway

#14 The Temple of the Ruby of Fire

#15 The Mona Mousa Code

#16 A Cheese-Colored Camper

#17 Watch Your Whiskers, Stilton!

#18 Shipwreck on the Pirate Islands

#19 My Name Is Stilton, Geronimo Stilton

#20 Surf's Up, Geronimo!

#21 The Wild, Wild West

#22 The Secret of Cacklefur Castle

A Christmas Tale

 #23 Valentine's Day Disaster

 #24 Field Trip to Niagara Falls

 #25 The Search for Sunken Treasure

 #26 The Mummy with No Name

 #27 The Christmas Toy Factory

 #28 Wedding Crasher

 #29 Down and Out Down Under

 #30 The Mouse Island Marathon

 #31 The Mysterious Cheese Thief

 Christmas Catastrophe

 #32 Valley of the Giant Skeletons

 #33 Geronimo and the Gold Medal Mystery

 #34 Geronimo Stilton, Secret Agent

 #35 A Very Merry Christmas

 #36 Geronimo's Valentine

 #37 The Race Across America

 #38 A Fabumouse School Adventure

 #39 Singing Sensation

 #40 The Karate Mouse

 #41 Mighty Mount Kilimanjaro

 #42 The Peculiar Pumpkin Thief

 #43 I'm Not a Supermouse!

 #44 The Giant Diamond Robbery

 #45 Save the White Whale!

 #46 The Haunted Castle

#47 Run for the Hills, Geronimo!

#48 The Mystery in Venice

#49 The Way of the Samurai

#50 This Hotel Is Haunted!

#51 The Enormouse Pearl Heist

#52 Mouse in Space!

#53 Rumble in the Jungle

#54 Get into Gear, Stilton!

#55 The Golden Statue Plot

#56 Flight of the Red Bandit

The Hunt for the Golden Book

#57 The Stinky Cheese Vacation

#58 The Super Chef Contest

#59 Welcome to Moldy Manor

The Hunt for the Curious Cheese

#60 The Treasure of Easter Island

#61 Mouse House Hunter

#62 Mouse Overboard!

The Hunt for the Secret Papyrus

#63 The Cheese Experiment

#64 Magical Mission

#65 Bollywood Burglary

The Hunt for the Hundredth Key

MEET
Geronimo Stiltonord

He is a mouseking — the Geronimo Stilton of the ancient far north! He lives with his brawny and brave clan in the village of Mouseborg. From sailing frozen waters to facing fiery dragons, every day is an adventure for the micekings!

#1 Attack of the
Dragons

#2 The Famouse
Fjord Race

#3 Pull the
Dragon's Tooth!

#4 Stay Strong,
Geronimo!

Don't miss any of these Thea Sisters adventures!

Thea Stilton and the Dragon's Code

Thea Stilton and the Mountain of Fire

Thea Stilton and the Ghost of the Shipwreck

Thea Stilton and the Secret City

Thea Stilton and the Mystery in Paris

Thea Stilton and the Cherry Blossom Adventure

Thea Stilton and the Star Castaways

Thea Stilton: Big Trouble in the Big Apple

Thea Stilton and the Ice Treasure

Thea Stilton and the Secret of the Old Castle

Thea Stilton and the Blue Scarab Hunt

Thea Stilton and the Prince's Emerald

Thea Stilton and the Mystery on the Orient Express

Thea Stilton and the Dancing Shadows

Thea Stilton and the Legend of the Fire Flowers

Thea Stilton and the Spanish Dance Mission

Thea Stilton and the Journey to the Lion's Den

Thea Stilton and the Great Tulip Heist

Thea Stilton and the Chocolate Sabotage

Thea Stilton and the Missing Myth

Thea Stilton and the Lost Letters

Thea Stilton and the Tropical Treasure

Thea Stilton and the Hollywood Hoax

Thea Stilton and the Madagascar Madness

Don't miss any of my special edition adventures!

THE KINGDOM OF FANTASY

THE QUEST FOR PARADISE:
THE RETURN TO THE KINGDOM OF FANTASY

THE AMAZING VOYAGE:
THE THIRD ADVENTURE IN THE KINGDOM OF FANTASY

THE DRAGON PROPHECY:
THE FOURTH ADVENTURE IN THE KINGDOM OF FANTASY

THE VOLCANO OF FIRE:
THE FIFTH ADVENTURE IN THE KINGDOM OF FANTASY

THE SEARCH FOR TREASURE:
THE SIXTH ADVENTURE IN THE KINGDOM OF FANTASY

THE ENCHANTED CHARMS:
THE SEVENTH ADVENTURE IN THE KINGDOM OF FANTASY

THE PHOENIX OF DESTINY:
AN EPIC KINGDOM OF FANTASY ADVENTURE

THE HOUR OF MAGIC:
THE EIGHTH ADVENTURE IN THE KINGDOM OF FANTASY

THE WIZARD'S WAND:
THE NINTH ADVENTURE IN THE KINGDOM OF FANTASY

THE JOURNEY THROUGH TIME

BACK IN TIME:
THE SECOND JOURNEY THROUGH TIME

THE RACE AGAINST TIME:
THE THIRD JOURNEY THROUGH TIME

LOST IN TIME:
THE FOURTH JOURNEY THROUGH TIME

MEET GERONIMO STILTONIX

He is a spacemouse — the Geronimo Stilton of a parallel universe! He is captain of the spaceship *MouseStar 1*. While flying through the cosmos, he visits distant planets and meets crazy aliens. His adventures are out of this world!

#1 Alien Escape

#2 You're Mine, Captain!

#3 Ice Planet Adventure

#4 The Galactic Goal

#5 Rescue Rebellion

#6 The Underwater Planet

#7 Beware! Space Junk!

#8 Away in a Star Sled

#9 Slurp Monster Showdown

#10 Pirate Spacecat Attack

Meet
GERONIMO STILTONOOT

He is a cavemouse — Geronimo Stilton's ancient ancestor! He runs the stone newspaper in the prehistoric village of Old Mouse City. From dealing with dinosaurs to dodging meteorites, his life in the Stone Age is full of adventure!

#1 The Stone of Fire

#2 Watch Your Tail!

#3 Help, I'm in Hot Lava!

#4 The Fast and the Frozen

#5 The Great Mouse Race

#6 Don't Wake the Dinosaur!

#7 I'm a Scaredy-Mouse!

#8 Surfing for Secrets

#9 Get the Scoop, Geronimo!

#10 My Autosaurus Will Win!

#11 Sea Monster Surprise

#12 Paws Off the Pearl!

#13 The Smelly Search

#13 The Smelly Search

ABOUT THE AUTHOR

Born in New Mouse City, Mouse Island, **GERONIMO STILTON** is Rattus Emeritus of Mousomorphic Literature and of Neo-Ratonic Comparative Philosophy. For the past twenty years, he has been running *The Rodent's Gazette*, New Mouse City's most widely read daily newspaper.

Stilton was awarded the Ratitzer Prize for his scoops on *The Curse of the Cheese Pyramid* and *The Search for Sunken Treasure*. He has also received the Andersen 2000 Prize for Personality of the Year. One of his bestsellers won the 2002 eBook Award for world's best ratlings' electronic book. His works have been published all over the globe.

In his spare time, Mr. Stilton collects antique cheese rinds and plays golf. But what he most enjoys is telling stories to his nephew Benjamin.

1. Main entrance
2. Printing presses (where the books and newspaper are printed)
3. Accounts department
4. Editorial room (where the editors, illustrators, and designers work)
5. Geronimo Stilton's office
6. Helicopter landing pad

THE RODENT'S GAZETTE

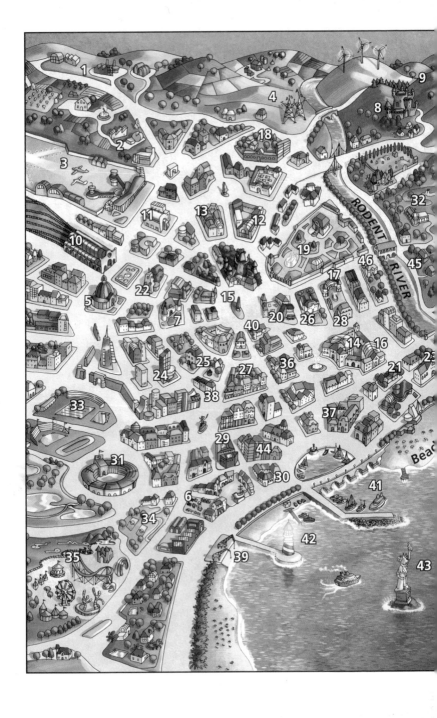

Map of New Mouse City

1. Industrial Zone
2. Cheese Factories
3. Angorat International Airport
4. WRAT Radio and Television Station
5. Cheese Market
6. Fish Market
7. Town Hall
8. Snotnose Castle
9. The Seven Hills of Mouse Island
10. Mouse Central Station
11. Trade Center
12. Movie Theater
13. Gym
14. Catnegie Hall
15. Singing Stone Plaza
16. The Gouda Theater
17. Grand Hotel
18. Mouse General Hospital
19. Botanical Gardens
20. Cheap Junk for Less (Trap's store)
21. Aunt Sweetfur and Benjamin's House
22. Museum of Modern Art
23. University and Library
24. *The Daily Rat*
25. *The Rodent's Gazette*
26. Trap's House
27. Fashion District
28. The Mouse House Restaurant
29. Environmental Protection Center
30. Harbor Office
31. Mousidon Square Garden
32. Golf Course
33. Swimming Pool
34. Tennis Courts
35. Curlyfur Island Amousement Park
36. Geronimo's House
37. Historic District
38. Public Library
39. Shipyard
40. Thea's House
41. New Mouse Harbor
42. Luna Lighthouse
43. The Statue of Liberty
44. Hercule Poirat's Office
45. Petunia Pretty Paws's House
46. Grandfather William's House

Map of Mouse Island

1. Big Ice Lake
2. Frozen Fur Peak
3. Slipperyslopes Glacier
4. Coldcreeps Peak
5. Ratzikistan
6. Transratania
7. Mount Vamp
8. Roastedrat Volcano
9. Brimstone Lake
10. Poopedcat Pass
11. Stinko Peak
12. Dark Forest
13. Vain Vampires Valley
14. Goose Bumps Gorge
15. The Shadow Line Pass
16. Penny Pincher Castle
17. Nature Reserve Park
18. Las Ratayas Marinas
19. Fossil Forest
20. Lake Lake
21. Lake Lakelake
22. Lake Lakelakelake
23. Cheddar Crag
24. Cannycat Castle
25. Valley of the Giant Sequoia
26. Cheddar Springs
27. Sulfurous Swamp
28. Old Reliable Geyser
29. Vole Vale
30. Ravingrat Ravine
31. Gnat Marshes
32. Munster Highlands
33. Mousehara Desert
34. Oasis of the Sweaty Camel
35. Cabbagehead Hill
36. Rattytrap Jungle
37. Rio Mosquito

Dear mouse friends,
Thanks for reading, and farewell
till the next book.
It'll be another whisker-licking-good
adventure, and that's a promise!

Geronimo Stilton